Secretly Inside

Library of World Fiction

Secretly Inside

A Novel

Hans Warren

Translated by
S. J. Leinbach

With an introduction by
Jolanda Vanderwal Taylor

The University of Wisconsin Press

This publication has been made possible
with financial support from
the National Endowment for the Arts

NATIONAL
ENDOWMENT
FOR THE ARTS

and from the Foundation for the Production and
Translation of Dutch Literature

The University of Wisconsin Press
1930 Monroe Street
Madison, Wisconsin 53711

www.wisc.edu/wisconsinpress/

3 Henrietta Street
London WC2E 8LU, England

1   3   5   4   2

Printed in the United States of America

Library of Congress Cataloging-in-Publication Data
Warren, Hans, 1921–
[Steen der hulp. English]
Secretly inside: a novel / Hans Warren; translated by S. J. Leinbach;
with an introduction by Jolanda Vanderwal Taylor.
p.   cm.
ISBN 0-299-20980-6 (hardcover: alk. paper)
I. Leinbach, S. J.   II. Title.
PT5880.W33S713   2006
839.31′364—dc22   2005021511

For

YTEKE and **BERT BAKKER**

Secretly Inside

Introduction

Jolanda Vanderwal Taylor

Hans Warren, a fixture of the literary scene in the Netherlands since 1946, died in 2001 at age eighty after a long
illness. Warren was known for his prolific work in a
wide range of literary genres, including poetry, published diaries, translations, and literary reviews. This
variety reflects a voracious curiosity. Warren started
writing reviews as a young poet, and had published several thousand articles in the *Provinciale Zeeuwse courant*
(the Provincial Newspaper of Zeeland) by the time of
his death. His reputation was most firmly associated
with his published diaries, a series entitled *Geheim dagboek* (Secret Diary) that appeared from 1981 on and
that rates as one of the twentieth century's most honest
and revealing sustained memoirs. Seventeen volumes
have been published to date; the fifteenth, covering the

period of 1982–1983, was published in 2000. The next volume, comprising a larger-than-average 352 pages, which deals with the last year of Warren's life, saw posthumous publication in 2002. Early 2004 saw the publication of the volume of *Geheim dagboek* that covers the years 1984–1987.

Hans Warren was born on 20 October 1921, in Borsele, Zeeland, a province in the southwestern corner of the Netherlands, which is made up in large part of islands, and was thus—particularly in the first half of the twentieth century, but even to this day—a relatively remote area of the Netherlands. Warren was an introverted and quiet child, who was interested in nature and poetry early in life. The *Geheim dagboek* series reflects Warren's broad interests. It established his reputation as a diarist who offers frank self-disclosure (often shockingly so, especially to his early readers) and analysis. His narratives and reflections upon his personal life included descriptions of his early marriage (a union he entered into despite his homosexuality), his life in Paris with his wife and three children, and their subsequent divorce. He came out as gay in 1975, the year *Steen der hulp,* or *Secretly Inside,* was published, and began his relationship with Mario Molegraaf in 1978. The diaries reflect on his friendships and professional relationships with many Dutch writers, and thus provide significant insights from Warren's personal point of view into the Dutch literary world. A recurring topic of the diaries was the beauty of nature in Zeeland and its peril as the area became less isolated from the rest of the world. During World War II, Warren published pieces in illegal (underground) publications, and after the war he frequently contributed to literary journals. He also published many volumes of poetry. His 1969 collection titled *Tussen hybris en vergaan* (Between Hubris and Decay) may be seen as representative of his literary interests; this volume foregrounds the tension between vitality and awareness of decline, which is also an ongoing theme in *Geheim dagboek*. Mario Molegraaf was forty years Warren's junior when they met. It is often said that Warren felt that this relationship helped him regain his vitality and sense of youth. Warren and Molegraaf successfully collaborated on translations of the work of many poets; the considerable reputation in the Netherlands enjoyed by the Greek poet Cavafy can be attributed to their efforts.

The novel *Steen der hulp* is Warren's contribution to a well-known strain of post–World War II narratives in Dutch literature: novels, short stories, and autobiographies that tell of hiding during the Nazi Occupation. Warren's version alludes to many traditional themes in this literature, most of which have some basis in historical fact; Warren's novel also includes an autoerotic theme, which was much less common at the time. A brief review of some salient facts in the history of World War II in the Netherlands will help the reader understand the theme of hiding as presented in literary works such as *Steen der hulp*.

The Netherlands had remained neutral during World War I and had hoped to do the same during any war Hitler might start. Hitler had guaranteed the neutrality of several European countries, including the Netherlands in August of 1939. While the government and many citizens hoped for the best, however, the Netherlands nevertheless mobilized its troops a few days later, just before the German attack on Poland. Any remaining hope for neutrality was undermined in January of 1940, when a German military plane made an emergency landing in Belgium and was found to contain plans for attacks on Belgium, the Netherlands, and Luxemburg. Most Dutch citizens, confused by the mixed signals, and bereft of any truly viable options, continued simply to hope that war would not come. Many Jewish citizens of the Netherlands, whose families had lived there for generations, even centuries, also remained in the country during the period preceding the war—some because they were confident in light of Dutch history that they would be safe, others because economic and international political realities denied them any realistic alternatives.

The surprise attack on the Low Countries finally came at 4 AM on 10 May 1940. The small armed forces of the Netherlands, a nation that had previously counted on a system of water defense structures—instantly rendered useless by the introduction of airplanes as military equipment—were wholly inadequate to the task of defending the country against the German assault, and the Netherlands capitulated on 14 May. In the meantime, the royal family and the upper echelons of the Dutch government moved to relative safety in London, from where they intended to guide the nation, while in fact leaving the Netherlands to be ruled by a civil government installed by the Nazi occupiers. This government attempted to gain control of the populace by waging a hearts-and-minds campaign while gradually introducing its racist and anti-Semitic policies, each stage accompanied by measures of intimidation and threats that resistance would be punished severely. These attempts to control the population were largely successful; the incremental introduction of anti-Semitic measures made each step seem relatively harmless to the ethnic Dutch, who were simultaneously motivated to accommodate by the increasing penalties imposed on those who resisted. By the time the principled and brave began to be organized, those who were willing to risk their families' safety and economic well-being for the sake of illicit resistance to Nazi policies, the vast majority of the Jewish citizens had been deported to transit- and concentration camps; it was, in a sense, too late for many. In all of Europe, the Netherlands had the worst record for survival of Jews who were citizens or residents at the beginning of the war: some three-quarters of them were murdered. Some of the reasons for the relative failure of resistance have already been mentioned. In addition, the resistance was hampered by the landscape, size, and population density of the country (there were few opportunities and places to hide, or to escape notice while engaging in illicit activities); by the nearly complete and remarkably accurate residence records maintained at city halls across the country; and by the willingness (for a broad variety of reasons) of Dutch citizens to betray to the Nazis their fellow human beings—whether Jews or (alleged) members of the resistance—in return for rewards or favors, or simply because they wanted to ensure the safety of their own families. As a result, various Dutch citizens and residents attempted to go into hiding in the Netherlands. Anne Frank, for example, whose *Diary of a Young Girl* became known around the world not long after the war, went into hiding with her family and several unrelated people in a building in Amsterdam that her father had physically adapted for the purpose ("remodeled" does not seem quite the right word for the Spartan accommodations this project yielded). Anne's father had carefully arranged in advance for the all-important support staff who would see to the family's needs by buying and delivering food (no easy feat in a time of scarcity and high prices, and also rationing supervised by the Nazis), and even providing reading material. This arrangement meant that the Frank family was able to stay together, and that they were not living with their helpers; this somewhat limited (but did not eliminate) the danger they posed to others. In some cases, where hiding places were betrayed, the victims would know the identity of the snitch, in others, like the Franks and their household, it would remain a mystery to them and their friends.

A perhaps more typical hiding arrangement required that families split up, and "farm out" individuals to other households (often to strangers) elsewhere in the country—indeed, often on farms, where food was less scarce, and space and privacy were more available than in crowded cities. Such arrangements might be made by those who wished to hide, either for themselves or for family members, or they might be made on behalf of others by members of resistance groups. These resistance groups established networks of individuals willing and able to help in various ways: locating a hiding place (often in someone's house), obtaining food, or arranging for false identity papers for refugees.

In light of the history of World War II, it should be no surprise that hiding from the Nazis becomes a theme of various literary genres in the Netherlands both during and after the war. There are many reasons for the popularity of tales of hiding, including a natural interest in recent history, the humanitarian appeal of such stories, the excitement associated with stories promising a life-or-death outcome, and, especially at first, a desire to believe the Dutch had strongly resisted the occupation, or a need to accuse them of a lack of fortitude.

Within this type of story, a range of settings and levels of fictionality should be expected. The most famous narrative about hiding in the Netherlands, Anne Frank's *Diary,* was written while she was in hiding, and, most poignantly for the reader, unaware that she would not survive the Shoah. While Frank did indeed edit and rewrite her work in the hope that it would be published, others wrote simple diaries, and published them after the war, with only minor editing.

An example of an additional type of texts of hiding with which Warren was certainly familiar is the work of Marga Minco, who, as a young Dutch Jewish woman, had gone into hiding during the occupation and found herself to be nearly the only survivor of her entire family at war's end. Minco published a number of different fictional stories and short novels, beginning in 1957, all of which present a variation on this theme. The main characters are typically young Jewish women who hide during the war under various circumstances (typically separated from their families) and in the end discover themselves to be alone, or nearly alone. As the decades pass, Minco's subsequent novels follow the lives of different but similar survivors further into the future. Not long after the war, she tells of survival and its aftermath, the shock of discovering that one is without family. A few decades later, the survivor deals not just with the initial implications of such a discovery, but also with the vicissitudes of memory and survivor's guilt. Minco's stories are deceptively simple in their style and language; her genius resides in her ability to adapt the basic heartbreaking tale to various times in history—and different periods in the survivor's life—and to present many variations in her theme.

Minco's work allows one to discern a number of common themes in the tale of hiding. One such theme, of course, is that of danger and insecurity. To the person about to go into hiding, danger is all around. Often, the main character goes to an unknown address (sometimes with the help of an unfamiliar guide), where he or she will be dependent on an unfamiliar host family for safety. The main character has no choice but to take on faith that everyone involved in arranging and carrying out these transactions will prove to be reliable. The same trust is required in situations where people in hiding are offered false identification papers—the early versions of these were unfortunately poorly crafted, yet people often had no choice but to stake their lives on them. Sometimes helpers turned out to be reckless, or even explicitly tried to take advantage of their charges, whether financially or sexually. The situation is further complicated by the fact that those hiding could be equally dangerous to their helpers, if they turned out to be reckless or traitorous; the penalties for assisting those in hiding were severe.

Warren places his narrative squarely within the tradition of Dutch hiding narratives. For a Dutch reader in the postwar period, the setting is delineated with elegant efficiency. The writer establishes the time, place, and context in just three brief sentences. The story begins as the main character is walking toward the house where he will attempt to "hide" more or less in plain sight from the Nazi occupation while taking on an alias, and with the understanding that the town's mayor is "trustworthy," or sympathetic to the anti-Nazi resistance. As he walks, he recalls the instructions he had been given; these simple sentences begin the novel, easily communicating to the reader an instant sense of the tension the protagonist must feel and the danger he could be in: "'When you've passed the last house of the village, turn right at the dike. You'll come to a very long lane that leads to the farm.' That was all he had been told." These simple sentences quite eloquently communicate a fair amount of information to the reader: the main character is looking for a location that is new to him. He has never been there before, and he most likely has never met his hosts. The setting is rural. The instructions are vague, leaving plenty of opportunity for anxiety, and perhaps danger, should the protagonist lose his way, or knock on the wrong door. The next sentence, which refers to the darkness, reinforces the reader's anxiety as well as his sense of familiarity with the scene. The protagonist is walking to an unfamiliar location after nightfall. He is on an illegal errand, because he is out walking around after the early-evening curfew, and it is dark not just because of the rural setting, where streetlights would be scarce, but also because of the blackout imposed by the Nazi occupiers. Energy sources were in limited supply, but the Nazis decreed nevertheless that all windows be covered with black paper to prevent any light from showing, so that Allied bombers could not use visual cues as they navigated

toward German targets. Warren's protagonist, remarkably, has a flashlight, but he does not dare turn it on.
Fortunately, after taking stock of his somber, melancholy mood, and after noting how hollow his footfalls
sound, and fearing that he may have lost his way, he
turns on the flashlight and recognizes the farm nearby.
As he approaches, he notices that the windows are
poorly blacked out—a kind of sloppiness perhaps toler-
ated in the countryside—and is able to observe his
hosts. In yet another signal to the reader that he is at
some distance from home or at least people of his own
class, it is noted that he can hear them speaking in a dialect he has trouble understanding. (It is important to
note that one did not need to travel *very* far in most areas
of Europe to hear an unfamiliar dialect of one's own
language.) He understands enough of the conversation
among the family members, however, to learn that they
have ambivalent feelings toward him—they are willing
to help, but they know that they would be safer without
his presence in their house. The narrative balances their
concern with ambivalent feelings on his part: he finds
the absolute peace and quiet attractive, and yet he fears
what will happen to him in this place. Again and again
the author confirms the rural nature of the location: the
deep silence, the fact that the front door is stuck shut
and has no doorbell (our hero knows enough about
country life to realize—after trying the front door—
that country folk would use the back entrance), the
wooden clogs lined up near the door. The reader finds

customary elements of stories of the resistance or of hiding during World War II, for example, the visitor has been given a password with which to identify himself; the host's short, stocky build, his face "dull brown in color, ravaged and sensuous, but also sly, with something criminal about it," and his "Mediterranean eyes," which "had a fierce glow" and "shot fire," on the other hand, do not fit the typical expectations for this kind of literature, and invite questions on the reader's part. To some extent, these questions are answered later, but throughout the novel, they contribute to a sense of other-worldliness, unpredictability, and uncertainty, and thus to the protagonist's feelings of fear.

Entering the house, the protagonist sees a large, poorly furnished and untidy room, which he studies for hints about how to fit in with "the family he would be a part of" for an indefinite period of time. The lady of the house is described as wearing traditional dress, appropriate for her place in a rural setting; her mourning dress, on the other hand, is unusual. However, the motherly benevolence she exhibits must be comforting to the visitor. In light of this characterization, the children are not entirely what one would expect: the daughter, Mariete, has black eyes and hair; the son, Camiel, has an olive complexion and a feminine mouth; he is wearing shabby, torn, too-small clothing. The visitor, having noted that the interior of the room is dilapidated, compares the family to gypsies, and is puzzled because he had been led to believe that the family was rich. The narrative continues with familiar elements of narratives of hiding: the dimly lit room, and a frightened protagonist.

Mariete, who has noticed the good material of the "visitor's" jacket, is apparently convinced that he is of sufficiently high class to recognize quality, and she shows him a dress she has made of expensive wool material. He tactfully identifies the object as being very valuable, and reads her diplomas, which she displays for his comment. Her father interrupts, calling him "Ed"—the first time the reader hears his name. One then learns that his name is Eduard van Wyngen, but—as those familiar with the genre expect—one is immediately reminded that this name will soon have to be forgotten. The reader is informed of his reason for hiding, as he recounts for his hosts that "until recently, when it was no longer possible, his father had been a teacher at a *gymnasium* in Utrecht, and that he hadn't just come to the farm to be safe from the reprisals that threatened him because of his origins and an act of resistance he had committed, but that he also wanted to work as hard as he could, to earn his place on the farm." He continues by thanking the people for their willingness to take him in, despite all the dangers. Now the reader knows for a fact that he is Jewish, and that he has been active in the resistance, and that he most likely is being sought by the Nazis.

Ed attempts to find out about the family whose house he now shares. From time to time throughout the novel, the text seems to reflect the chaotic situation, the danger of the times, and the main character's lack of access to information crucial to his survival. While the reliability and trustworthiness of his hosts—each member of the family individually—is of the utmost importance to him, there is no way he can be sure of them. The narrative reflects his uncertainty of how to interpret what he sees around him; he seems to change his mind frequently, leaving the reader with his or her own confusion about the facts and about their proper interpretation. The text emphasizes differences in sub-culture that exacerbate the difficulty of understanding his surroundings: he is Jewish, his hosts Roman Catholic; his background is urban, and he has come to the country; he is educated and middle class, they are—allegedly wealthy—farmers, but not highly educated.

Ed attempts to get his bearings in his new surroundings by asking about the farmer's origin—he is told the family is from Spain. He is, of course, hungry, and the farmer's wife offers him food: porridge, bread, lard, and salt ham. The cultural differences are underscored when the narrator observes that it had not occurred to the farmer's wife to wonder whether these foods were kosher, "because she had never heard of such a thing"; then, in a nice reversal, the narrator indicates that Ed does not keep kosher, making the point moot. Yet another indication of such differences appears when Ed begins to eat: his hostess asks him whether he eats like the animals, then tells him: "Religious or not, as long as

you're here in my house and at my table you'll pray before you eat, and don't forget it." And then, somewhat
embarrassed: "Or don't you Jews pray?" thus indicating
to the reader that she is aware that he is Jewish. He explains that his family is not religious. He then bows his
head and folds his hands silently, in a gesture she finds
acceptable.

Having just established the religious differences
between the two parties, the text now turns to class and
secular subculture: Ed is given an unwashed cup (pos-
sibly recently used by a sickly cat) from which to drink.
The text makes his unease clear, while indicating that
Camiel does not think twice about such matters. Then
the narrative turns to the contents of Ed's suitcase. The
scent of his clean clothing is a reminder of his home,
which now seems far away; his clothes are not appropriate for work on a farm. A greater problem, however, is
with his books. It is clear that he will have to give them
up, as they are in English and French and, if the house
were searched, they would endanger the family by revealing that he is out of place—although one of the
books has a Roman Catholic imprimatur. In a peculiar
scene, the farmer's wife then offers Ed a missal—"You
can use this book. Then at least you'll have something
to read. It's not your religion, but it can't do any harm.
It belonged to my mother, for whom I'm in mourning.
She died this spring." This gesture seems downright peculiar, but at least her statement answers Ed's question,
and that of the reader, about why she is in mourning.

The situation becomes even more awkward when the farmer begins to complain—in front of his new guest—about that fact that they have not yet received any proceeds from his mother-in-law's will, and then proceeds to express the wish that his ill sister-in-law will die before the inheritance is distributed.

When his wife responds with understandable pique, he attempts a conspiratorially sexist comment toward Ed: "I wouldn't get on that woman's bad side, if I were you." The narrative mentions that Ed bows his head in a silent prayer of thanks for the meal he has just eaten (a common practice among Dutch Christians of the time), but the reader may well wonder whether he does not also include a supplication for his well-being; he must have some feeling of despair after the recent scenes, which raise doubts about the family's common sense and even sanity.

Later, Camiel shows Ed his treasures: a double-barreled hunting rifle and two pairs of skates (figure skates and speed skates). Ed, of course, knows the rifle to be illegal, but he does not know why Camiel has it. Camiel discusses a number of private matters with Ed—that he brushes his teeth only once a week, and has a cavity—once again emphasizing his rural character and simple lifestyle—that he has a girlfriend who means nothing to him, but whom he feels he will have to marry to provide labor (hers, and their children's) for the farm. Camiel's confused and confusing attitude is underscored when Ed states that he would like them to become good friends—but Camiel demurs, apparently frightened: "You shouldn't talk about that. [. . .] I don't always know what I want. Don't ask me too much. I don't make any plans, don't promise anything anymore. . . . You remind me too much of someone. I'm scared." The text reveals that Camiel's tone frightens Ed; one would think the message would frighten him, too, as it reveals Camiel to be completely traumatized by some past experience that he is unwilling to discuss. While traumatic experiences are not uncommon in wartime, this does not seem a typical event, and Camiel's mental state is of central relevance to Ed's safety. Danger comes from a variety of potential sources. Where traditional hiding narratives often emphasize the danger of the neighbors' prying eyes, as well as those of business associates and passers-by, in this novel the local population is left unmentioned—presumably because it poses no danger. (But how can Ed trust that this is true?) Nevertheless, in this novel, the danger seems to reside as much within the household as beyond it. The family members have presumably pledged themselves to protecting Ed's safety, but they seem not to be in control of themselves. What further occupies Ed and concerns the reader is his attraction to Camiel, and Mariete's apparent—but ambivalent—attraction to him.

The first night, Ed falls asleep, has disquieting dreams, and—the reader no doubt sees this coming—wakes up to find that Camiel and his rifle have disappeared, although he returns before dawn. The next morning, Ed further investigates his surroundings. When at breakfast, noticing his hosts seem even less pleasant than the night before, he decides that the relatively unpopulated world outside must be safe. The farmer tells Camiel that Ed is to stay out of sight until he has his new papers, but "out of sight" in this case seems to include the great out-of-doors on the farm. While this relative freedom should be reassuring, new details about the family undermine the reader's sense of Ed's safety: Camiel talks about two of his sisters with serious mental problems that he attributes to inbreeding. The narrative again emphasizes the differences between the two worlds, in this case the varying meanings of wealth in the city and in the countryside.

Ed, who has begun to feel a fondness for Camiel, now reverses the equation of security; where most narratives of hiding express anxiety about the safety of the person in hiding, Ed now wonders whether his presence endangers Camiel. His sense of security is undermined because Camiel is different from Ed's friends, and by his discovery that these country people are nothing like what he had expected. Ed, in leaving his world for a world of hiding, has lost all his bearings. Becoming infatuated for what seems like the first time only clouds his judgment. The text indicates repeatedly that he can no longer trust his instincts, or his ability to judge the relative safety of a given situation.

In the evening, Ed and Camiel go to the mayor's house in the village and rather casually invent a fake identity; false papers are made up almost immediately for Ed. Certain details, such as birth dates, are left basically unchanged whenever possible; others need to be altered. For example, Ed is registered as a Roman Catholic farm hand. These developments are cause for concern by the reader: there are certain things Ed will need to learn soon, lest he be exposed. Camiel is unconcerned, however, and as the text intones, he trusts "in the loyal cooperation of the town council and the villagers." As if to tempt fate, Camiel decides that they will go straight to a café in the village. Unsurprisingly, Ed has difficulty fitting in there because of regional and class differences, even when he attempts to cover up by making some crude remarks. He would, however, have been more successful if he had known how to play pool well, or been familiar with any of the locally popular card games.

An odd conversation ensues: Ed wonders aloud why Camiel does not go after what he wants in life. He points out that Camiel does what he doesn't enjoy, and that he has a girlfriend he doesn't love; but then he realizes that his question is unwise, as it seems that "the night already had Camiel in its grasp." Ed senses (though he cannot see) that Camiel "had that same frightening look he had the night before" and tries to encourage him to go home, but Camiel responds with a mystifying outburst: "I've got nothing to do with you. I don't care if you do look like him." Ed attempts to follow Camiel into the night, and comes upon a mysterious scene. Someone else may or may not be there. At home, he is told that Mariete is out, and the reader wonders whether she was the other presence Ed had felt outside. Feeling increasingly alienated, Ed attempts to summon the image of Isabel, his girlfriend, but is unable to do so; he is isolated from his normal world. The text suggests that he feels a new, wistful desire for a religious attitude that he has not embraced: "At moments like this Ed sometimes wished he could pray."

The text offers an explanation of the book's original title: the name of the farm is Eben-Haezer, or "Stone of Help." Above the mantelpiece there is a fresco depicting an angel. Ed talks with Mariete, who adds to his sense of alienation when she discusses her plans for the future, her parents' marriage, and the mysterious events in Camiel's past that have so traumatized him. Confusion persists, however, as there is no indication concerning whom to trust and whom not to trust. Mariete is going to marry an older, unattractive, literally dirty man for his money, to avoid being alone, and because she is the last of her circle of friends to remain unmarried; he is a man of her class, and his farm is doing well enough. She tells Ed about her pilgrimage to Rome and Lourdes, and a trip through Spain, where she visited the area where her ancestors had lived. After he has decided for himself that she is "a strange girl," she leaves and returns in a flamenco costume complete with castanets, to dance and sing for him. When her behavior turns expressly (and somewhat insistently) flirtatious, he seems to respond, but refuses to kiss her, explaining that neither of them is "free," and that they both "have to live here together for a long time." She responds, somewhat ominously, and, he thinks, maliciously, that it might all be over soon. When he inquires what she means, she refuses to explain, but comments that her home is a "madhouse," referring to strange things that happen at night, and warning him to watch out for Camiel, whom she describes as "weak." "Her voice sounded sincere, familiar, but her gaze was demonic and inscrutable," states the narrator. She explains that Camiel had had a friend who committed suicide—except that he had been "a Kraut" (German), and that no one had really believed that it had actually been suicide. Camiel and the friend had met in a café: "they were together round the clock, no matter how much father would rant and rave about it. And he knew far less than I did." She points out that Ed looks a lot like the "Kraut," and states that it's strange that he, a Jew, and the "Kraut" look alike. She explains that she had found the suicide victim, half-dressed, and wearing lipstick, which she reports wiping off; and she persists in her attempts to make Ed kiss her.

Later, Camiel explains that his lover, though a soldier, was not a German, but rather Viennese, an anti-Nazi named Ernst. They did not talk much because Camiel's German wasn't very good, but they had an understanding. Ernst wrote poetry and read it to Camiel. The end came when Ernst learned that he had been transferred to the Eastern Front and announced that he wanted to die, but was afraid to commit suicide. He asked Camiel to kill him; when Camiel refused, a fight ensued; Camiel—who claims to have lost his memory of the events—apparently killed Ernst by accident. Since then Camiel has suffered from his memories, and now is traumatized because of Ed's resemblance to Ernst.

Ed values peace and quiet: inner serenity in harmonious surroundings—but, contrary to his expectations, he does not find it in the country. "Mariete desired him, but he had no interest in her." She reveals to him the desperate marital situation of her parents—they don't love each other, but have learned to tolerate and appreciate each other, and they never go out together. They did only once; on that occasion, they were badly injured when they drove into a tree, leaving the husband with a concussion, and the wife with a leg injury that has never quite healed. The children are traumatized by their violent arguments. Mariete describes herself as dangerous, and implores him to leave "before it's too late," stating that he has no idea what she is capable of. She attempts to seduce him; he refuses more clumsily than he intends to because he cannot think of a gracious way out.

Ed's attempts to work show him to be an incompetent farm hand. Camiel seems calmer since his outburst of a few days earlier. Ed senses danger—he is afraid of Mariete and decides to leave the farm as soon as possible. He asks Camiel's advice, who agrees that Mariete is dangerous, as he suspects she has a German boyfriend on the side; he arranges to meet Ed later that evening to help him escape for a while. Ed is irritated that his safe house has turned out to be unsafe. However, before they can get away, the police raid the house. Ed and Camiel leave through a window; as they run away, Camiel is wounded by gunfire and has to remain behind. Several years later, after the end of the occupation, Ed returns to the house to inquire after the family. He finds that they all were punished for protecting him. The house has been destroyed. He sees only Camiel, who is dressed as a soldier, and speaks broken German; he is mentally sick with grief over the loss of his loved ones. He produces a ragged, bloodstained scrap of paper containing a fragment of a poem of love and longing. The poem is "Einem der vorübergeht" ("To one who passes by") by Hugo von Hofmannsthal, which was written at the time of his first meeting with Stefan George, and thus points beyond the novel to a famous "real-world" homoerotic affair expressed in poetry.

In the end, Warren's brief novel is a compelling contribution to a well-known body of literature. He uses many themes common to works that deal with hiding in the Netherlands during World War II, but he also adds his own creative twists. The somewhat unusual theme of homoeroticism is not in the least as utopian as presented here; it participates in all the same problems — such as confusion and danger — that characterize the depiction of life under the Nazi occupation within this tradition. The novel conveys a shifting, amorphous reality in progressions of scenes whose structures are more cinematic than novelistic. The result, though, is a work that shares themes and characteristics with the rest of Warren's writing. The unsparing approach displayed here is consistent with the author's prevailing tone. He never prettifies his characters even when, as in his diaries, they were literally his loved ones, and one writer, himself.

One

"When you've passed the last house in the village, turn right at the dike. You'll come to a very long lane that leads to the farm."

That was all he had been told.

It was so dark that he wasn't even sure if he had already passed the last house, but then he saw the turn-off, the cart tracks littered with small white shells that vaguely showed the way. They crunched under his shoes. To avoid making any sound, he stepped onto the wet grass between the tracks, which disappeared into the darkness under a tunnel of trees.

Darkness and silence enveloped him. The almost leafless treetops formed indistinct silhouettes against the overcast night sky.

He shifted his suitcase from one hand to the other and stumbled into one of the ruts.

He would have liked to switch on his flashlight, but he didn't dare. The marshy smell of dead leaves and withered spearmint put him in a melancholy mood.

Even after walking a few hundred of yards he still didn't see any sign of a farm. The path began to slope downwards, and a dense white wall rose up in front of him: a pocket of mist above a creek that gently licked the woodwork of a bridge with white railings.

His footfalls sounded hollow on the planks, so he went the rest of the way on tiptoe, uphill, out of the mist.

The lane stretched on endlessly, like a black shaft.

Finally, wondering if he had completely lost his way, he risked turning on the flashlight.

He pointed the beam of light straight ahead and was reassured. About two hundred yards away the glow was reflected in a window pane.

The darkness was made even more dense by all the bushes beneath the trees, but suddenly, without having passed a fence, he found himself at the edge of a farmyard, the boundaries of which dissolved into the night. A few slender shafts of light and a poorly blacked-out, heart-shaped figure in one of the shutters betrayed the location of the farmhouse. Rising up in front of it were four old, manicured lindens. He put down his suitcase under one of them to gather his courage before ringing the bell.

Flanking the front door were two tall windows.

The living quarters were apparently on the right side. He heard voices and loud radio music. Through a chink in the inside shutters he saw the broad back of a girl who was reading a magazine. He also saw a piece of brown oilcloth, a dirty cup, and a little pile of sticky pear skins.

The high-pitched, somewhat nasal voice of a boy and the related, but creakier voice of an older man were quarreling in a dialect he could scarcely understand. The speakers were outside his field of vision. The girl at the window looked up from her reading. He only saw the back of her head, which was spiny due to all the metal curlers sticking out of her black hair.

"Mother . . . *Mother* . . . you can't hear yourself think with that radio on. Can't you turn it off? . . . *Mother,* he's late, don't you think?"

He picked up his suitcase; it was now or never.

The rather indifferent, almost masculine voice of a woman replied calmly, "Oh, I'm sure he'll come, and if he doesn't, that's fine too. That'll mean less trouble for us."

He couldn't find a bell anywhere, and the doorknob wouldn't budge.

It occurred to him that in the country people usually went in through the back door, and so he walked around the house. It proved to be a wide, almost square building, completely separate from the barn.

A slight shift in the cloud cover offered him a

glimpse of the surrounding area: a sizable plot of land, full of buildings and outbuildings and trees. Absolute peace and quiet, everywhere.

In part this attracted him; in part he feared his future here. With a shuddery motion he literally shook all the thoughts out of his head and lifted the smooth, iron knocker.

The back door yielded to his touch, and he shouted, "Is anybody there?" He called out a second time, but nobody heard him; the radio inside drowned out every other sound.

He tripped over the threshold, stumbling his way over the wooden clogs and sacks that lay strewn across the entryway. The smell of the place was bitter, as if animals lived there. He was startled by a cat, which soundlessly slipped past him on its way outside.

Again he called out, but once more there was no answer.

Then he closed the door behind him and switched on his flashlight.

He found himself in a large, bare, vestibule-like room with a speckled granite floor, surrounded by six brown doors, a pile of dirty, muddy sacks and a multitude of wooden clogs with initials burnt into the tops. In a corner there was a small water filter on a pink stool.

He took a chance and opened one of the doors. Behind it was a hallway, and he could hear the radio more clearly.

Once again, at the top of his lungs, he called out.

"Hey, hush up, I hear someone," said the old, slightly nasal voice. "Turn the radio down."

A moment later the door to the room opened. A little multicolored dog followed the lamplight into the hallway, yapping excitedly.

A short, stocky man appeared in the doorway, and even in the shadow cast by the visor of his cap, his eyes had a fierce glow.

The visitor gave the password, and the farmer nodded brusquely.

"Van 't Westeinde."

The little dog was friendly. It was already leaping up at the visitor, its tail wagging back and forth.

"Come on in," said the man, gesturing with both hands at once. His face was dull brown in color, ravaged and sensuous, but also sly. There was something almost criminal about it. It was a gruesome, wrinkled mask, and yet traces remained of once-handsome lines, and the Mediterranean eyes still shot fire.

Two

He entered a large, badly furnished, and untidy room. An oppressive odor of food and people, fumes from the oil lamp, and noxious smoke from the wood-burning stove made him want to cough. Newspapers, rags, and calico cats covered the floor. Hanging from the ceiling beams were sausage wreaths, rows of hams, and sides of bacon. Around the table with the standing oil lamp sat three people: the farmer's wife, a daughter, and a son.

So this was the family he would be a part of.

Keenly wanting to fit in, he locked eyes with each of them as he shook their hands. In the light the father turned out to be less decrepit, but more corrupt, than he had first thought. His eyes, which were encircled by countless wrinkles and long lashes, had an unruly charm. The fine, droopy lips formed a sneering grin around a thoroughly ravaged set of teeth. His posture had also been neglected; he was paunchy and stooped, which made the short, heavy-set man appear even more squat.

The lady of the house, in traditional dress, got up from her armchair to greet him. Resting against the chair was a cane. It took some effort for her to come to her feet on account of her stiff leg, but when she finally managed to stand, she cut an impressive figure, large and robust, majestic in her mourning dress.

She had a plump, colorless face and black hair that was almost entirely tucked away under her small lace bonnet. The lines on her face, which was still beautiful at middle age, betrayed willpower and ambition and a hint of breeding, and the sharpness of her sober gray eyes was tempered by a motherly benevolence. Her deep voice was nonchalant, rough and not unfriendly.

The visitor immediately felt drawn to her.

Mariete, the daughter, looked to be in her late twenties. She was stout, too. Curious black eyes sparkled at him from a pretty, broad face, framed by jet-black hair. Glistening with droplets of sweat, a noticeable moustache shaded her lovely mouth. Each word she spoke in her lilting voice revealed two rows of gleaming, flawless teeth.

It was hard to say how old the son was. Camiel could have been eighteen, but he could just as easily have been twenty-four. Short like his father, well built, olive-colored, and beardless. Also a Mediterranean type; they looked like a family of gypsies.

Camiel had strange, somewhat squinty eyes, with long, curly lashes that came up to his thick eyebrows. The excessively plump, rather feminine mouth and his hesitant, wandering gaze disturbed the harmony of his face.

Their clothing could not have been shabbier. Apart from the mother they were all wearing rags. The farmer, who doffed his cap every so often to audibly scratch his close-cropped gray hair, wore a brown jacket, the lining of which was sticking out every which way. Mariete had on a ridiculous, short, faded dress, which revealed her fat, bare thighs whenever she bent over, and Camiel's shoulder stuck out through a large tear in his soiled blouse.

The visitor found this odd, because he had been told these people were rich.

The interior was also dilapidated.

Worn-out mats on the floor, stained wooden chairs, two deep, appallingly grubby tub chairs of a now inde-terminate color—the dog was lying on the one, and salt continually dripped onto the other from a side of bacon hanging above it—and a table with a sticky sheet of canvas nailed to it: that was the extent of the furnish-ings. There was also a large, shiny cabinet on which milk glass vases glowed in the dim light, and a speaker for the radio rediffusion.

It was hard to make out what was hanging on the wall, as the circle of light did not reach that far. Only directly across from him, between the windows, there was a beautiful Louis XVI mirror, in which the visitor saw a full-length reflection of himself: a city boy, a student, his clothing smart, in these surroundings almost elegant.

He was extremely pale, but with his hair and his big black eyes, he made a darker impression. He looked frightened: what am I doing here?

Eager and fearful, he absorbed all this in a few moments, trying to realize where he had ended up. Then he quickly turned away from his own reflected likeness.

Three

Four faces were turned towards him in the lamplight, all of them with questions.

"Well, you look like a strapping lad, at least," said the farmer.

"Can you work?"

"I'm not used to farm work, of course, but I'll do whatever I can."

Between her thumb and forefinger Mariete approvingly examined the material of his jacket, which the visitor had taken off on account of the warm stove.

He saw that she was wearing an engagement ring.

"I bet you don't think I've got any nice clothes. I don't bother about that around here. I don't have to get all dressed up for the crows and the magpies. On the farm I wear things till they fall apart. But what do you think of this dress . . . ?"

She dashed out of the room, came back to fetch a flashlight, and presently returned with what was in fact a very nice dress, made of supple black wool.

"What do you think this cost, my friend?"

To flatter her, he guessed, "A hundred-fifty guilders."

She laughed with a twinkle in her eyes.

"Do you really think so? You're a man of the world, eh? I bet you've got to beat the girls off with a stick. And I'm sure your mother and sisters have nice things too. You know your prices. . . . Did you all hear that? . . . A hundred-fifty guilders he says, and he knows what he's talking about . . . for the crows and the magpies. . . . No, it cost a third of that. Just the material. I do all the rest myself: the design, the sewing. Surprised, aren't you? Look . . ." And with that she nervously grabbed a roll of crumpled papers out of a drawer of the cabinet, "Here are my diplomas."

Loyally and attentively he read over three certificates, which stated that Miss Maria Joanna Apollonia van 't Westeinde had passed her courses in dressmaking, fine lingerie, and fashion design with honors. He rolled them back up, and slightly astonished, but also amused, he considered the problem of whether the newly completed dress, which was now draped over Mariete's body, needed the silver corsage that she coquettishly held up to her shoulder. He thought it was better without, while Mariete, who was now arranging herself in front of the mirror, preferred it with, but then her father angrily pushed aside the fashion magazines and the box of swatches she had brought with her.

"First we need to talk. You and your dresses all the time. Do you think Ed cares about that stuff?"

Mariete was visibly hurt by her father's remark but said nothing. The visitor gave a concise summary of the essentials. They knew his name, Eduard van Wyngen, but that name would have to be forgotten, and quickly. He said that he was twenty-five, studied literature and for his pleasure psychology, that he had a girlfriend named Isabel, that until recently, when it was no longer possible, his father had been a teacher at a *gymnasium* in Utrecht, and that he hadn't just come to the farm to be safe from the reprisals that threatened him because of his origins and an act of resistance he had committed, but that he also wanted to work as hard as he could, to earn his place on the farm. He also thanked the people for their willingness to take him in, despite the danger.

"Before I forget: you've got to go to the mayor's tomorrow. I've arranged it. Completely trustworthy. Camiel will take you there after dark. In the meantime you're going to have to entertain yourself around here," said Van 't Westeinde. After that it was his turn. And so he launched into an endless series of hunting stories, punctuated with exuberant gestures and dreadful grimaces. His whole manner was so exotic that Ed asked him if his ancestors had come from the south of France, as was the case with many people in that region.

"Spain!" cried Van 't Westeinde enthusiastically and proudly. "Our forefathers were Spaniards."

"My mother's mother was also Spanish," said Ed quietly. The farmer wasn't listening and went on excitedly.

"We've got an old family album with all the names in it. Woman, where is that book . . . ?"

"That's for another time," said the farmer's wife. "And now you're going to shut up about your poaching expeditions because I want to say something, too, for once. Have you eaten, my boy?"

Ed was awfully hungry and said so.

"There's still a pan of porridge. Camiel always eats a bowl before he goes to bed, and I'll cut a few slices of bread for you too. Mariete, the bread!"

She rummaged around in the table drawer for the knife, held the enormous loaf of bread against her bosom, and deftly began cutting it into slices, thin ones, perfectly formed. She put them in front of him on the table, with a dish of lard and a few slices of salt ham.

The fact that this might not have been entirely kosher did not even occur to her, mainly because she had never heard of such a thing. Nor could she know that it didn't matter, not in Ed's case.

He was about to dig in, but she asked imperiously, "So you eat like the beasts in the field, do you?"

He looked up, dumbfounded, and she seemed to sense resistance, because she then added: "Religious or not, as long as you're here in my house and at my table you'll pray before you eat, and don't you forget it!"

And then, somewhat embarrassed: "Or don't you Jews pray?"

"At my house we're not at all religious," he said quietly, "even though . . ." But he left out the rest, and thought: what does it matter? No point in making a fuss over something of no importance.

He folded his hands and bowed his head for a short time. The radio was turned down for the purpose.

"Now that's more like it. Eat hearty," said the farmer's wife when he looked up again.

Nonplussed, he ate his porridge and bread. The bottom slice had to be pulled loose from the oilcloth with a tearing sound. All the while a sickly cat eyed his cup of milk, the same dirty cup that was already sitting on the table.

Meanwhile, Mrs. Van 't Westeinde asked what kind of clothes he had brought along.

"Overalls?"

"Two, and a pair of corduroys, and smocks. Just have a look in my suitcase," and he gave her the keys. He stole a glance at the neat little piles, hastily packed by his mother. The soft, salutary fragrance of the linen from home suddenly wafted through the pungent air of the farmhouse room, and the smell made him sentimental for a moment. The farmer's wife expertly unpacked everything. She laid the underwear in the cabinet with their own underclothes. The rest of the clothes were put on hangers in an unused box bed, which gave off an unbearably strong odor of mothballs when she opened the small doors.

Little was left in the suitcase: toiletries and two books, which he had packed because he was in the middle of reading them when he had to leave: *A High Wind in Jamaica* by Richard Hughes and *Sur le devoir d'imprévoyance* by Isabelle Rivière.

Mrs. Van 't Westeinde glanced through the books. Although she could not read them, he saw an expression of satisfaction appear on her face when she saw that the book by Isabelle Rivière had an imprimatur as well as an inscription with a carefully drawn cross and the letters PAX above it.

She did not put them back.

"This must be a good book," she said. "We're Roman Catholic too, you know."

Ed had already gathered that from the gold cross in the hollow of Mariete's throat and the crucifix surrounded by artificial flowers with a devotional lamp in front of it which was dimly visible in a dark corner.

"But these books, my boy," the farmer's wife continued, "are dangerous in this house. We don't have books like that here, and if they come to search the place, and unfortunately it wouldn't be the first time, they make us suspect."

Ed understood that he had lost his books. The

farmer's wife searched through a drawer of the cabinet for a missal that was bursting with devotional pictures and other pious papers and put that in his suitcase.

"You can use this book. Then at least you'll have something to read. It's not your religion, but it can't do any harm. It belonged to my mother, for whom I'm in mourning. She died this spring."

"When are we going to see our share of that inheritance?" the farmer suddenly blurted out. "We're supposed to be in that woman's will, you see. She had a few million, and my wife has four sisters and a brother. By the way, what's going on with your sister? If she's going to die, she'd better do it now, before the inheritance is divided up."

"She's getting better. You should shut your mouth and stop talking nonsense!"

The farmer looked at Ed with an expression of feigned fright, his eyes bulging out like a chastened schoolboy's. He lifted his cap and scratched his head again.

"I wouldn't get on that woman's bad side if I were you," he grinned.

Ed bowed his head to say a prayer of thanks for his dinner.

Meanwhile Camiel had also polished off his porridge, which he had shared with a fat white tomcat.

He had said virtually nothing the whole time, now and then faintly and benignly smiling at his father's stories, which he must have heard a thousand times before.

Mariete remained in a foul mood, eventually wishing everyone a curt good night and disappearing upstairs.

"We're all going," said the mother.

"Tonight you'll have to sleep with Camiel. Tomorrow you'll get your own bed."

Four

Camiel's room was located on the main level, but it had a raised floor that put it partially above the cellar vault. Half the space inside was occupied by an old-fashioned double bed.

They got undressed by the light of a candle.

Camiel showed Ed his treasures: a double-barreled hunting rifle and two pairs of skates, figure skates and speed skates. Apart from those things, Camiel's wardrobe and room were empty but for some clothes and a few slightly damaged porcelain figurines.

The gesture he made as he showed off the rifle and skates touched Ed. He tried to fathom the loneliness of these four hard, self-centered people.

Mariete with her dresses, the father with his memories, the mother with her struggle to prevent the religious dissolution of the family, and now the taciturn Camiel with his dearest possessions, especially the illicit rifle.

"You must be quite a rider."

"I'm all right, I guess."

Ed saw the uncared-for, dirty hands as they caressed the immaculate greased horseshoes and the painstakingly cleaned, supple leather.

It was as if Camiel felt it. "Do you always cut your nails?" he asked naively.

"Of course, how do you keep yours short?"

"They just wear down on their own. I only have to cut them in the wintertime, when there isn't much work."

There was no place for him to brush his teeth, only the large enamel chamber pot under the bed. Camiel got a cup of water for him from under the filter, while Ed lit the way.

"I only brush my teeth once a week," said Camiel. "I've got a hole in one of my back teeth, and I'm afraid to go to the dentist. Can you see it?"

He gave Ed a small mirror and made all sorts of faces. Ed maneuvered the dripping candle but saw nothing, only—oddly enough—that the youth already had a shock of very thick, snow-white hair above his ears. Finally he discovered the unsightly hole in the molar. Otherwise Camiel's teeth were small and perfect, though the ones in the back were covered in plaque. He smelled quite nice actually: warm and sandy. A comradely atmosphere began to develop between the two of them.

He is childish and neurotic, thought Ed, but I like him.

When he climbed into bed next to him, he asked, "How old are you anyway?"

"Twenty-two."

"Have you got a girl?"

"Yes, but she doesn't mean anything to me."

"So why do you stay with her?"

"Cause I have to. You know, for the future. Mariete is getting married next year, and then mother is going to be all alone on this big farm with her game leg."

"You could always hire a maid, couldn't you?

"I don't know, strange people in the house . . . and it's so expensive."

"Your family has money, right?"

"Yeah, but I've still got to get married, some day. I can't stay on my own on a farm like this. It's a big help to have children who can work for you when you get older—just look at father. He doesn't do anything anymore. He leaves everything to me and the farmhands."

Ed sympathized with this boy who seemed so resigned to his fate. He himself was a rebel; only sometimes he was brought to his knees by unjust circumstances. It was not in his nature to give up without a fight, even though it might have been the wise thing to do. And to what extent had he resigned himself to his own absurd fate, to be cast off and persecuted for being something he was not, for a nonsensical notion that had assumed insane proportions?

"Camiel?"

"Yes."

"I want us to become good friends."

"You shouldn't talk about that."

"Why not? Why couldn't it happen?"

"I don't always know what I want. Don't ask me too much. I don't make any plans, don't promise anything anymore. . . . You remind me too much of someone. . . . I'm scared."

Ed was startled by the tone of his whispering.

"I've got to get my rifle."

Camiel nimbly sprang over him, and Ed caught a whiff of the pungent odor of fresh perspiration.

Camiel put the double-barreled rifle against the wall next to the head of the bed.

A short time later Ed thought he heard Camiel sleeping.

He himself had trouble falling asleep. Far, far away he heard a sort of murmuring, like the sea, and the sinister hooting of an owl echoed over the farmyard at regular intervals. His thoughts wandered off in all directions. Even so, he eventually nodded off.

An impressive, glossy eagle with a white rosette on its chest alighted high atop a bare tree.

The evening sun gilded the barkless branch and the bird, transforming them into a stately monument against the colorful sky.

Camiel took aim. There was the sound of a shot, the proud white chest turned red, and the bird plummeted to earth, falling from branch to branch.

Feathers fluttered poetically through the air.

He awoke with a start, the echo of the shot still in his ears, and he listened, horror-stricken and perfectly still in the pitch darkness.

No breathing betrayed Camiel's presence.

Cautiously he felt to one side.

Camiel's place was empty.

The rifle was gone from the head of the bed.

He shivered with emotion as he lay there; the slightest sound pierced deep into his eardrums.

After what seemed like an eternity he heard footsteps in the grass, and later at the back door.

Was there whispering?

Shortly after that the door opened quietly.

He couldn't make out anything in the dark, but the room was soon filled with the damp smell of autumn.

Camiel mumbled as if he were dreaming, took off some clothes, and lay down very carefully next to him. It was clear that he did not want to disturb Ed any more than was absolutely necessary, and Ed did not dare show any sign of being awake.

Camiel shivered so violently that the bed shook, and his teeth chattered as he gasped for air.

Very slowly the shivering diminished, and a pleasant warmth began to permeate the bed so that they both fell asleep, exhausted.

Five

The next morning he had a chance to do some exploring and see where he had ended up. It was a quiet, sunny October day. The soft light that fell across the breakfast table robbed the family of much of the charm they had had by lamplight.

Mariete was busy and in a snippy mood. Behind his paper, farmer Van 't Westeinde was brooding about a transaction in town. The farmer's wife was quiet, and Camiel stared out absently over the farmyard.

In front of the house there were expansive, irregular lawns covered by groups of trees whose bronze, semi-leafless crowns seemed closer due to the large nests in their branches made by herons and rooks.

The faded green was dotted white and pink by small groups of sheep and geese and a few free-ranging pigs. The boundaries of the property were obscured by the many trees and shrubs. Here and there Ed could see a patch of pasture with spotted cows or harvested fields, but that was all.

It seemed like an extremely desolate, safe area.

Before Van 't Westeinde left, he impressed upon Camiel how important it was that Ed stay out of sight until his papers were in order.

"Go plough today in the gallows nook, and let Ed pick apples in the orchard. He'll be safe there."

Outside was the pungent smell of autumn. The sky twinkled with groups of migrating titmice as they flew by, high in the rarefied air. Now and then a sonorous cry bubbled forth from the spasmodically swelling throat of a dark red, robust rooster, whose mighty warble was answered by higher voices elsewhere on the farmyard.

The outbuildings stood together in a loose cluster: the tall, long barn with its thatched roof and adjacent dung pit, a cowshed on the other side of the same pit, a pigsty with the outhouse built against it, a carriage house, a large shed or summer cottage, and a milking house. It was a small settlement, peaceful and cut off from the rest of the world.

From far away, the deep tolling of a church bell broke through the downy silence.

"That's the Kruisdorpe parish church, where you got out yesterday," said Camiel.

"So how far is that from here?"

"Two miles or so. The lane alone is a mile long."

"And the closest farm?"

"Over yonder. It belongs to my Uncle Kees."

He drew aside the twigs of the hedge, and beyond the apparently endless, bright green beet fields, Ed saw the red tile roof of a barn protruding from a clump of trees.

As if Camiel guessed his thoughts:

"Two of my sisters couldn't take it here. One ran away; no one knows where she is now. The other one is in the Sancta Maria Sanitarium, a madhouse. Inbreeding. Money marries money. The land has to stay in the family. We try to acquire more, if we can, like this farm. It was bought from Protestants who couldn't keep it going. Over there, at my uncle's place, six out of eight of them are completely or half crazy, including my aunt, his first cousin. Almost all the farmers in these parts are uncles or cousins of ours. We're proud, no man's inferior. We're free. We look down on people with obligations, guys like you, who become teachers or go to work for a newspaper and get stuck in a dead-end job, at least if their parents haven't got any money. You can write, can't you? D'you know I can hardly write? I've never written a letter. Are your parents rich too, Ed? Yes, of course they are."

With a dreamy, childlike expression on his face, he gazed out over the land.

Ed's parents weren't the least bit rich, but he felt that Camiel would irrevocably lose whatever respect for him he might have if he were to confess that.

"*Ach,* rich . . ." he said, "probably not as rich as yours, but we do all right."

And it occurred to him how posh life at his house would seem to Camiel.

He cast a sidelong glance at Camiel, and a spontaneous, warm feeling welled up inside him for that unstable, naïve youth.

Wasn't he—by his mere presence, simply by being who he was—already doing him harm?

One wrong word, and an abyss opened up which could swallow up not only Camiel but also anyone close to him.

There was something dangerous and mysterious inside him. The strange, uncertain look in his eyes (green-gray in the daylight) contained a warning, which he had already sensed when they first met.

Ed was on the alert: idealistic enough to want to help Camiel, skeptical enough to know that help was probably futile, even if he really did start to care for Camiel.

Until that day, all his friends had come from his own limited circle, people he had gone to high school with, fellow college students. Even in that group there were some very strange characters. More than anything it was the atmosphere of artificiality, which partially spoiled even his relationship with Isabel Vlaming, that so often palled on him. It was so far from what he felt to be simple and true that their life together was starting to seem like a sham, kept alive by constant self-deception.

He had formed an idea about country folk. He had expectations of a purer environment, the one comfort of his exile. But last night he had noticed right away that the family he had ended up with was a far cry from anything he had imagined.

Six

They came to a watering hole for the livestock, a pond surrounded by pollard willows. At the place where the animals came down from the pasture, the muddy bank had been trampled by hooves, but the other banks were high and grassy and asked to be sat upon.

A black-and-white heifer was taking a drink and dreamily raised her head as they approached. The droplets fell back into the water from her rough snout, and the ripples on her reflection expanded into ever-wider circles until they touched the weather-beaten red water lilies.

Slender goldfish glided past beneath the sunny surface, and a green frog leapt wildly over the duckweed. Woodpigeons chattered away in the willows.

They sat against a split, rough tree trunk, which was bursting with ferns.

The surroundings were too idyllic.

A white horse walked slowly past. Camiel had a lump in his throat when he said, "Look, Bertus has lost one of his shoes."

Ed followed the fluid gait of the massive animal, watched the sunlight glide over its white back and leg muscles and felt the tension subside.

Camiel shot him an inscrutable glance. There was something shadowy, something incomplete about his face.

Ed now felt strange and limp, like a person feels after an attack of vertigo. He briefly thought about Isabel, and something in his consciousness shifted. He slipped into a landscape that had nothing to do with what his eyes were seeing. It was so harmonious and familiar that he reached out towards it in a kind of divine longing. Feelings from primeval times, from ancient ancestors, gave him a sensation of recognition and security, a happiness so great and yet so painful that he had seldom experienced anything like it, in dreams or in life.

He must have foolishly stretched out his hands towards that image, because he noticed a grip around his wrists, and the lines of the landscape gradually coincided with the features of Camiel's face, which was right above him. The dark woods with the wind whispering through them were his hair, the undulating, ochre hills his cheeks, the red and white bands of flowers along the arid field, his mouth, and the lake in which he blissfully and deliberately drowned, his eyes, looking at him anxiously and shyly. The exotic, southern landscape of his soul was captured in that countenance. It stirred up dark emotions, caused a spring to well up inside him, a spring he had never supposed existed. Feelings, hitherto unknown to him, yet so familiar that they must have always been there, sealed away as if in a reservoir, like a gift passed from one generation to the next. Were these the unseen Andalusian fields his grandmother had told him about when he had sat at her deathbed, his hand in hers?

Camiel said nothing, asked nothing, and Ed said that he was a bit dizzy, weary after yesterday's journey, the emotions, all the new things.

"How did your family get such a thoroughly Dutch name?" he asked.

"It was changed, probably as far back as the French period. Our ancestors were named De Claramonte, and they came from Linares, at least that's what father claims. I don't know if it's true. I don't much care, really. It doesn't interest me. Mariete is more attached to tradition. She even went to Spain to have a look around." Ed deliberately looked at Camiel again, as he sat there. There was definitely something about him that reminded Ed of a character in a fairytale, the nobleman's son in rags. The face and the body betrayed race, strength, as well as an almost decadent refinement. His fingers were hard and black, with deep lines running through them. There was dirt in the folds of his ears. He had no beard to speak of, but apart from his very curvaceous mouth, there was nothing feminine about his face.

To break the spell, Ed stood up.

They walked through the orchard and the vegetable garden, surrounded by dense hawthorn hedges that were red from the berries growing on them. The air was heavy with autumn melancholy. Spider silk gleamed in the sunlight. Slowly, as if they were drunk, velvety, brightly colored butterflies danced above bursting fruit that had fallen from the trees.

They beat nuts out of a young tree that Camiel had planted as a child, and in no time Ed's hands were as black as Camiel's from the sap of the shells.

Camiel pointed out the apples he had to pick and the lean-to under which the baskets could be found.

Ed kept wanting to ask, What was all that about, last night? But he was afraid.

Seven

Cutting through the air like a siren, Mariete's voice announced that lunch was ready. Afterwards they went to work. When he was climbing around in an apple tree to pick the fruit at the top, Ed could see how Camiel made black furrows in the golden brown stubble field. In front of him three massive white horses strode forward in cadence, and behind him the air was alive with a flock of white seagulls that swooped down again and again behind the plow to pick up the worms that had been turned up.

Ed got tired of picking apples, but the work made him happy.

That evening they went into the village. With smiles on their faces, they invented the details of Ed's new identity at the mayor's house. They kept the information the same as much as possible.

Ed became Cornelis Goense, a relative of Camiel's mother who had been living in Utrecht. The birth date was kept the same, while his birthplace became Beekveld, a nearby village.

"They'll never check that," chuckled the gray, somewhat unsteady, rustic man.

With the help of an old-fashioned telephone, a little brown wooden cabinet with cranks and hooks, he asked a reliable official who lived in the neighborhood to come over, and he had him make false papers for Ed from their supply of stolen personal index cards and identity cards.

Camiel waited with the mayor, while Ed followed the official to his house. A yellow card full of information was speedily typed up—the man told Ed that every person has such a cardboard doppelganger from birth—and a blank identity card was filled in. For the second time Ed placed his inked fingertip on the back of a passport photo of himself, but now he was Cornelis Goense, farm worker, religion: Roman Catholic. He was given the identity card, and the index card would be placed in the civil register the next day.

Given that the Van 't Westeindes were not planning on keeping him hidden forever, especially now that he had the proper papers, and trusting in the loyal cooperation of the town council and the villagers, Camiel decided to give Ed the baptism of fire.

They went into a pub where a few men were playing cards and shooting pool, and he was introduced as the new farmhand. He had difficulty fitting in: he couldn't participate in their conversations or play pool well, and he didn't know their card games.

Camiel evidently felt at home there and tried to get Ed to join in, but he just toyed with the coasters and stared at the old-time advertising prints on the walls, one of which, depicting a crowned falcon above a romantic horizon, fascinated him. He felt miserable.

He was in danger of getting entangled in lies and so he said as little as possible. Nevertheless, he managed to win acceptance by affecting an attitude of extreme nonchalance and making a few daring, crude remarks.

He drank the bad, stale beer and then insisted that they go.

Camiel did not reproach him when they were back out on the street.

"Aren't there any games you know?" he asked.

"Oh . . ." he began. He wanted to say: I don't like going to pubs either, but instead he said, "I'd like it if you'd teach me to play pool better and show me some new card games."

"I don't really like it that much either, but what else can you do on a Saturday or Sunday? You can't sit at home all the time."

They had reached the dark lane, which was now a little more familiar to Ed than yesterday. He was tired and somber, and without thinking he blurted out:

"Don't you have any ambitions, any ideals? You've got a girl, and you don't love her. You go out in search of a good time, and you don't enjoy yourself."

Camiel laughed somewhat sheepishly. That painful laugh was his only response, and Ed didn't know how to make amends for his outburst. What was said, was said. He put his hand on Camiel's shoulder and tried to find words that would cheer him up, but before he could come up with anything, he noticed how the night already had Camiel in its grasp. He had that same frightening look he had the night before. Ed felt it, though he couldn't see Camiel's face very well. When they had passed the bridge, Camiel said:

"I don't want to go home. I'm going back," in a tone of voice that startled Ed.

"You have to come. We're nearly there, Camiel."

He felt how Camiel's shoulders were trembling before he pulled away.

"Oh, I have to, do I? Is that right? I've got nothing to do with you. I don't care if you do look like him. Let me go!" And when Ed followed him, Camiel let out such an animal scream that he stopped, his heart pounding, and heard the rapid rustling of Camiel's footsteps over the wet leaves as he ran into the orchard.

He didn't know what to do. How could he go back to the house, *his* house, now? For a long time he just stood there and listened to the lethal, damp silence. His heart calmed down. He called out Camiel's name a few times. He walked a short distance into the orchard, waving the flashlight back and forth. All to no avail: he had to continue on his own.

Before he went inside the house, he felt Fox's warm tongue licking the palm of his hand. He ran back with the dog to the spot where Camiel had disappeared.

"Go find your master!" he ordered the dog, but the animal just stood there between his legs. He went into the orchard and repeated his command. "Go on, Fox, go and find your master."

This time the little dog took off like a shot. For a brief moment he heard the speedy feet pattering over the ground, and then, far away, a series of short barks.

Following the sound, he came to a pile of woodcuttings and alder stumps in which there was an opening.

Fox leapt out of it when Ed approached with the light. Somewhat apprehensive, he shined the light inside.

Under the brushwood was a small, elongated hollow with a floor of dried leaves and ferns. Camiel was lying face-down on it, motionless.

Frightened, Ed switched the light off and then back on again. His shadow danced whimsically around the fantastic hollow. He said Camiel's name softly, touched his legs. Nothing moved. When his fear subsided he crawled into the warm little room under the wood and sat down on the leaves.

He secured the flashlight between the branches and turned Camiel's body around, talking all the while. Camiel didn't try to stop him. His face was a taut mask, and his glassy eyes were wide-open. There was dirt stuck to his lips and forehead. Ed's words washed over Camiel like a soothing stream. He cleaned the wet leaves and moss off his icy, tightly clenched fists, and warmed them in his own hands. Finally he dared to wipe the dirt off his face.

Maybe it was this almost motherly gesture that did it, because then the tears came, first gliding slowly out of the corners of his lackluster eyes, and then streaming down his face as his sobbing body convulsed.

Camiel turned away from Ed, and yet at the same time, it was as if he were reaching out to him.

"I'm so scared. Where's my rifle, Ed?"

"My name is Cornelis," Ed said in jest, as if he were speaking to a child. "Come along home. Hurry up. Your rifle is there too. They'll start getting worried if we're gone much longer."

Eventually Camiel let himself be persuaded, tender and groggy.

When they crawled out from under the wood, Ed thought he could hear the crackling of twigs, as if someone were retreating into a recess. Fox was on the alert too; Ed called him to his side. He waved his flashlight recklessly back and forth, but the only thing he could see were capricious sylvan fantasies with reddish yellow leaves that stood out sharply against the jet-black shadows.

It was sinister and frightening, not suitable for

calming strained nerves, and so they continued on in the dark, the dog running on ahead of them.

At home Camiel did not say a word. He plopped down in one of the deep tub chairs and closed his eyes as if he were asleep. Maybe he was.

Ed spoke loudly and extra cheerfully about their experiences in the village, the duration of which he stretched out in order to prevent questions. He asked where Mariete was.

"She's gone to bed, I think," said the mother. "Her suitor came by to return a horse he had borrowed, and she went part of the way back with him."

Ed could not fall asleep in the big bed in the attic, tired though he was. He was preoccupied by the experiences of the day. Everything revolved around Camiel. He wasn't any closer to unlocking his secret. Rather, he began to suspect even more mysteries in this house and in this family.

He heard the back door being slammed a few times. Then came the sound of a bucket of water being thrown outside and, finally, the door being barred for the night.

He would have liked to be with Camiel, in his room, and yet he was also glad that he was alone and could think clearly, without being influenced by the presence of another.

He tried to call Isabel to mind, to consult her. But her image refused to appear; he could not even remember the sound of her voice.

He felt uneasy.

Just as one could sense a thunderstorm approaching, so too, catastrophes often announced their arrival.

At moments like this Ed sometimes wished he could pray.

Eight

Eben-Haezer was the name of the farm. Stone of Help. Previous owners had given it that name ages ago.

The walls of the largest room were covered with paintings and photographs of the Van 't Westeinde family. Over the fireplace hung a primitive mantelpiece. Above it was a fresco depicting a decidedly feminine angel, dressed in green. She held a man-sized golden anchor in one hand and a palm branch in the other, and her eyes were raised dramatically skyward. She was standing in a colonnade with a black-and-white tile floor, and with her enormous wings, she almost appeared to be trapped inside the columns. The name of the farm was divided over the pedestals of the columns. It was practically illegible, because another name had apparently been there before, dating from an even earlier period, something with *Hope* in it. That explained the figure with the anchor.

The massive, partially defoliated lindens in front of the house made the room very dark, even in the late autumn, and the somber people in the portraits staring from the walls with their serious eyes created an almost sacred atmosphere.

Evidently no one ever used the room. Most of the green plush chairs were so moldered that you wouldn't dare sit on them.

One of the portraits showed Camiel's grandfather as a young man. His face appeared to float to the surface of a pool of glistening black water. In that same pool was a small coat of arms featuring a turret and little white horses. The face had large, bushy sideburns; otherwise it could have been a picture of Camiel.

Ed found himself in the room when he was helping Mariete peel apples for canning. She had gone to the pantry there to see how many jars of applesauce were left over from last year.

To make conversation, he asked her about her fiancé, a slightly older, gruff farmer he had once seen briefly.

"Do you think I give a damn about him?" she exploded. "What a pig! Sometimes I can't even stand to look at that stupid long face of his anymore, so I toss him out!"

"Why are you marrying him then?"

"He's got some money, he's good to me, and I'm sick of always being alone. I'm not old enough to stay at home if there's a party or a dance somewhere. If I could just resign myself to sitting here with father and mother and a pot of coffee, darning a sock. . . . But no, my friend, that's never going to happen.

"All my girlfriends are already married, and pretty soon I'll be thirty. This is my last chance. And my farmer is very good to me. He can't do without me. But don't think for a second that he's madly in love with me; I know better. His parents are dead, and he's got no female help at his place. He has to do all the cooking himself and manage the household with an apprentice farmhand. He needs a wife to take care of him, to mend his clothes and milk the cows. He could have done a lot worse than me, let me tell you. I'm not bad looking, am I? I've got money too—but I'm not getting married yet. Maybe I never will."

"Mariete, you're being stupid. I'd much rather stay unmarried than get tied down to someone I detest."

"Sometimes he makes me want to puke. Do you know he hardly ever bathes? Once a week he washes his face in the cow trough, and I don't think he ever washes the rest."

Ed looked mystified. This place was still stuck in the Middle Ages, when people walked around with shit stuck to their asses, like dungy sheep in the fields.

"Father says he chews tobacco too. I've never noticed it, but if it's true, I'm throwing him out!"

She said this with such force and conviction that Ed burst out laughing, falling onto one of the dilapidated plush chairs, which then collapsed, sending him to the floor. This only made him laugh even harder. By then Mariete was roaring with laughter too, and she started playing the clown:

"And he's stiff with rheumatism. When he gets up, he groans and coughs, and the sound is enough to make your hair curl. If I get fed up with him, I'll just run away. Then I'll come back here or go to work. I know what I'm doing. If I don't get married now, I never will. Besides he's a man of my class, and his farm is doing well, though the soil is a bit inferior to what we have here."

"Have you had other suitors?"

"Oh, yes. I was with one of them for five years. He was a cousin of mine. I was crazy about him, followed him everywhere, paid for everything for him, you know how it is. But he didn't care about me. He was so handsome. All the girls were crazy about him. He just took it as his due. He preferred race cars, and eventually he broke it off. I was a wreck. I had saved so much money, mainly by making clothes, which I also did for other people, because no one else in the village could.

"I had wanted to use that money to pay for part of my trousseau. Now that wasn't necessary. I had had it. I was on the verge of a nervous breakdown. We have that tendency in my family, you know. Then I took a trip, on my own. I wanted to see something of the world. Maybe it was for the best that I didn't marry Leo. There are enough nutcases in this family.

"I went on a pilgrimage to Rome and Lourdes, and I traveled around Spain. I wanted to see where we came from. In Linares I found gravestones with the name Claramonte—that's our real name—and a coat of arms like the one on some of the portraits there. God, it was all such a waste in the end. Now I'm here, and I'm going to marry that twit. Then it'll all be over. No more dreams for you, Carmencita de Claramonte!"

Ed looked at her as she stood there: dark, fiery, her fairly heavy body in a hideous, short, faded green dress, a dirty, multicolored apron in front and thick hand-knit stockings.

With her tattered slipper she kicked over the apple tub and uttered a heartfelt "Bah!"

"You don't look much like Carmen," he said, gently teasing her.

She looked at him with uncertainty. Was he really making fun of her? No, the look on his face was sweet, actually. Surprise ripened in her wild eyes.

"Wait here. Mother's not at home anyway." She was already undoing her apron. "Un momento, por favor . . ."

She was gone for a fairly long time. Ed thought things over. It was beyond his comprehension that a rich and not unattractive girl in her twenties had decided to agree to such a marriage, although he vaguely felt that his powers of understanding were inadequate, that her motives, like Camiel's, were real and that his surprise was superficial.

Still, Mariete was a strange girl.

The clicking of castanets echoed in the stone hallway. He jumped up, surprised at the rhythm. In this weird house anything was possible.

Humming a tune, Mariete swished into the room, sparkling and unrecognizable in black and red, an advertisement for Maja soap come to life.

High heels made her taller, the long tiered skirt and the high mantilla made her more slender. Her eyes blazed behind the fan. She sang and clacked to a dance he didn't know. Even so it was nice to watch, and it made his pulse race.

"You can't do it like this," she panted, repositioning a blood-red dahlia. "You need two people."

He looked her up and down, critically.

"Wow, don't you look stylish!"

He meant it admiringly, but he could hear that it sounded sarcastic. He regretted it; that wasn't his intention. Yet something sensual in her voice had embarrassed him.

Her face hardened, and her sunny mood suddenly darkened. A fit of anger turned her eyes ugly.

"You're just like all the rest, just as mean. . . . Besides, I did it for myself, not for you."

She took off the mantilla and put it next to the apples, along with the fan and the castanets.

74

"That's not the way I meant it, Mariete. I was surprised—I hardly recognized you."

"You're making fun of me. Of course you're used to better in the city. I'm just a stupid farm girl from the sticks!"

This coarse reaction was not genuine. He felt it and that was why it didn't bother him.

She had lifted up the beautiful lace skirt. He saw her well-formed ankles, enclosed by thin, black silk stockings. Her slightly sweaty scent titillated him.

"Mariete, you know perfectly well that's not how I meant it," he said pleadingly, as he placed his hand on her arm.

She smiled and came closer to him, although her body barely moved.

"What then?" she said enticingly.

Panicked and agitated, he tried to find some way of dodging the question. He came up with Isabel and her farmer, and he said quietly:

"I don't know."

"Do you think I'm pretty?"

"Yes."

"Why don't you kiss me then?"

"Because neither of us are free, and we have to live here together for a long time."

"Silly baby," she sneered. "All this might be over sooner than you think."

It sounded malicious, and it scared him.

"What do you mean?"

"I'm not going to say. But this place is a madhouse, don't you agree? Just watch your step. Haven't you ever heard anything? Have you ever noticed things at night?"

"No," he said, thinking of the few times he thought he *could* hear something.

"Watch out for Camiel," she said suddenly. "He's my brother, and he's a good kid, but he's weak. And it's a strange time. Sometimes you can forget that there's a war going on."

Her voice sounded sincere, familiar, but her gaze was demonic and inscrutable.

"I never forget there's a war going on," he said softly. "And what's wrong with Camiel?"

"A friend of his committed suicide. It happened a year ago. He was a Kraut, don't worry. He shot himself in the heart in our orchard. Father was furious. We were all locked up for four days, because no one believed the Kraut had killed himself. I didn't either, but there was no evidence, and they let us go. When we got home, half our house had been looted."

"Were there Krauts here?"

"There still are, in a position between Beekveld and here. It's a small group. They don't cause much trouble."

"How did Camiel come in contact with him?"

"Who knows, in a pub? The two found each other right away. They were together round the clock, no matter how much father would rant and rave about it. And he knew far less than I did.

"But to be honest, he was a nice guy. It's crazy, but you look a lot like him, Ed. A Jew who looks like a Kraut, and vice versa."

She laughed derisively. It was an unpleasant sound.

"He came here in secret, in civilian clothes. He'd never come to the house, of course, but I saw him a few times when he came to the orchard. That's where he and Camiel would meet.

"That's where he died too.

"He made a beautiful corpse. I found him when I went to pick apples. He was lying on his back, with blood on his chest and in his underwear. He was half-dressed. His lips were still bright red, which I thought was odd. I wiped them with my handkerchief. The red came off. . . . I didn't tell anyone about that. Now give me a kiss."

Reluctantly he pressed his mouth against hers, which opened into a ghastly abyss. Yet at the same time she excited him with her quickly moving hands.

Irritated, he pushed her an arm's length away from him, his hands around her shoulders. Her wet lips below the moustache repelled him, but her demonic eyes were enticing. What a story! He kissed her eyes, caressing them with his lips, so as not to have to endure that gaze any longer, and said:

"We have to peel apples, Carmen de Claramonte. So hurry up and turn back into Mariete van 't West-einde. Your father and Camiel will be here to eat soon, and there's coffee to be made!"

And then chance came to his aid.

Someone called out "Hello?" at the back door.

"You see who it is," she said. "I can't go in this dress."

It was a girl who had come for some eggs.

When Van 't Westeinde, Camiel, and the farmhand came in from the field to eat, she was peeling apples as if nothing had happened.

Nine

Camiel looked sick.

Black circles under his eyes, headache. In the afternoon he was in bed.

Mariete had gone to the market in the neighboring town with her father, who in his "Sunday best" looked like a cross between a farmer and a down-at-heel artist. Mrs. Van 't Westeinde had gone to visit her sick sister for a night.

To keep him company, Ed had sat in Camiel's room with some old newspapers, the only thing there was to read besides the prayer book.

Camiel was asleep. Ed looked at him over the edge of the paper. He kept grimacing, and his fingers clenched and relaxed.

All of a sudden he sat bolt upright in bed and slammed his fist against the edge of the bed so hard that he broke the skin.

He laughed at Ed, a self-conscious laugh.

Ed felt pity and affection and asked recklessly:

"What's going on? That first night, when I slept next to you, I noticed you went out at night. And later on, there was that business in the woodpile. What's going on?"

He didn't answer.

Ed was overcome by emotion. Should he be asking this? Was he tormenting Camiel? On the other hand: wasn't he himself in great danger here?

Maybe it was his swollen eyes that did it, because Camiel then put his hand on Ed's sleeve.

"I remember so little. I'm just afraid, always afraid."

"Does it have something to do with that German? Mariete . . ."

"Damn that girl!"

Camiel was clearly startled. His irises quivered and then went rigid.

"You can trust me. You know that, right?"

"There's nothing to tell. I don't remember much about him. He was a good friend. And he was no Kraut; he was Viennese. He was against the Nazis. You know the story, but that's how it was. It was nothing special."

Camiel's voice sounded harsh, almost sarcastic, and Ed saw in his face that he had resolved not to reveal anything.

His eyes wandered around the room with feigned indifference.

"Camiel, if it wasn't anything special, then why did you shoot him?"

With a mixture of dread and satisfaction Ed saw that he had hit the mark. Camiel turned ashen, and he intuitively reached behind him for his rifle.

Ed trembled and said nothing more.

Then Camiel began to cry, first soundlessly, then in uncontrollable sobs. Finally he stretched out on his back.

"Can I really trust you?"

"Yes, Camiel."

"Swear it, on the barrel of my rifle, while it's aimed at you."

Terrified and yet strangely composed, Ed acceded to his whim and placed his fingers on the double barrel, which Camiel pressed firmly against his chest.

He felt miserable and foolish, expected the shot at any moment, but it never came.

Camiel put the gun back and lay down again, and in a faltering voice, he began to tell his story.

As the only boy, the youngest child of a bad marriage, in a family where the rest of the children were girls, he had had a lonely and unhappy childhood. Of course, he was spoiled as a child, and as a good-looking youth he was somewhat girlish as well. The extremely remote location of the farm was also the reason he never had any friends as a boy and had become introverted.

Later, at the agricultural college, he learned to adjust to others a bit, but that remained superficial.

He talked and talked. Ed took note of various things and filled in incomplete thoughts, because much of Camiel's "story" was little more than near-incoherent rambling.

In the evenings, especially on Saturday and Sunday, Camiel would often play cards at a certain pub in Kruisdorpe, to kill time.

One evening a group of half-drunk Germans burst in and began making a nuisance of themselves. Except one of them: a dark, skinny youth, who seemed to be embarrassed by the boisterous behavior of his comrades.

The card players and the men at the billiard table got up and ostentatiously left the pub, and Camiel reluctantly followed.

The young German had given him a look, shy and friendly at the same time, and he had answered it, because he felt attracted to him.

"I knew it wasn't right, but there was something in his eyes that made me happy. I deliberately lingered outside by my bike, and what I had hoped for happened: the door opened and he came up to me. His name was Ernst. He was only there for a moment, as if he'd gone out to take a piss. He couldn't leave his group.

"My German wasn't very good, but we understood each other. He asked me where the pastor lived. I pointed out his house to him.

"'Would he see me?'

"'I don't know,' I said.

"'And you, aren't you afraid of being seen with a German?'

"'No,' I said, and that was the truth. With him, I didn't care. He asked me where I lived and wanted to know if he could come by some time.

"I said I'd like to talk to him, but that it was impossible for me to see him at the house. We arranged to meet in the orchard, and from then on he came regularly. We became friends.

"For the first time I had a friend, a friend I was proud of, even though I was supposed to be ashamed of him at home and around other people. We built a little room in the woodpile, and we used to sit there if the weather was bad.

"Although they grumbled about it a lot at home, they pretty much let me do as I pleased. Maybe they were a little scared, I don't know. We hung around together like that for a good six months, the whole summer long. It was the most wonderful time of my life. It was touching to see how careful Ernst was that no one ever saw him go into the lane.

"Most of the time he would come here in civilian dress, even though that was strictly forbidden. He wanted to cause me as little trouble as possible, he said—as if he had any control over that! But if he didn't come or if father was in a bad mood and I wasn't allowed outside, I was so unhappy.

"Ernst was a poet. He read verses to me. I don't know anything about poetry, but it sounded nice, and we enjoyed being together.

"One warm evening in October he came to me with the news that he had to go to the Eastern Front.

"We were sitting in front of a hedge, and both of us were feeling pretty low. It was still early in the evening, and the air was muggy, like a storm was on the way.

"We cut our initials in a perfect young tree trunk, and he suddenly drew a heart around them.

"He shouldn't have done that, it wasn't necessary.

"Then he put his arm around me and said that he couldn't live without me and didn't want to.

"I let him do it and said that I didn't know what we should do either.

"It was true, but I shouldn't have said it the way I did, because then he just lost control.

"'There's no future for me. I'll die on the Eastern Front. There's no getting around that. I want to die here, where I've been happy. But I'm a coward. I'm scared to do it myself. Here's my revolver. Everyone will think it was suicide.'

"He didn't even *ask*.

"'Selfish bastard,' I said. 'Then all of us here will get rounded up and maybe even shot because a Kraut was killed on our property. Besides, I can't do it. I love you.'

"'Do you really love me?' Ernst asked, and I don't remember what happened next. Honest to God, I don't. There's a permanent knot of misery and confusion in my head, a black hole in my memory.

"I only know that we fought, really fought. It was literally a life and death struggle, but now and then we would bite and kiss each other. Then we'd go on fighting, like savages, and when he really started crushing me and I felt myself suffocating, I reached out blindly and grabbed the revolver I suddenly felt beneath my fingers. Both of us had totally forgotten about it. With all the strength I could muster, I freed my right arm, pressed the barrel against his chest, and fired, triumphantly. I won, I had to live.

"He was killed instantly, of course, and in that same instant I sobered up. I tried to arrange everything so that it looked like suicide, and then I hurried home to clean up. After that I went off to the village, where I got drunk, hoping to give myself an alibi. The thunderstorm that had been threatening all day finally came and washed away any traces of what we did there . . ."

Camiel said nothing for some time and turned his head back and forth on the pillow.

"I heard the rest from Mariete," said Ed, "how she found him and what happened to all of you afterwards."

"Mariete, yeah, she didn't have an easy time of it either. The autopsy revealed certain unpleasant details, which they kept bringing up during the interrogation, like the fact that the victim had had an orgasm just before he died. . . . They kept asking the same questions.

Mariete didn't know anything. She couldn't do much more than guess, and I couldn't say anything. I just clammed up. She took me for a halfwit, small wonder in a family like this.

"I've never been able to confess it either. It's in my head, in my body, and now and then it's like it wants to break out, and then I lose my mind, Ed, I really do. At those times I *am* crazy. It happens every night, especially in October, and it's been even worse since you came, because you look so much like him."

There was a long silence.

"Say something, Ed."

But Ed didn't know what to say. Anything he could think of would be dangerous, wrong or, at the very least, futile. It would be best just to leave. This wasn't a good place for him.

"You want to live now, don't you? You think that life is worth living, right?"

"No, now I want to die too. On my motorcycle, in the car, drinking, fighting . . . I seek danger everywhere. I take chances. I really don't care about anything anymore. Sometimes . . ."

"Yes?"

"No—forget it. It's gone."

Through the window they saw Fox start to wag his tail and take off across the lawn like a shot.

"Your father and Mariete are coming—you know what I swore to you, Camiel."

Ten

There was really nothing Ed valued more than peace and quiet: inner serenity in harmonious surroundings.

He was most strongly aware of that during those rare moments when he could consciously taste that peace, with its autumnal flavor of transience. The effect was invigorating, and yet somehow did nothing to disturb his glorious idleness.

When he was still living in the city, he had thought that, if nothing more, he would find that beneficent atmosphere in the country.

Instead, the days at Eben-Haezer were unsettled, a torturous mixture of restlessness and uncertainty.

Mariete desired him, but he had no interest in her.

He noticed it the second time when they were going through the family photo albums together.

A whole clan of rigid, exotic faces in their high-buttoned Sunday clothes stared at him from the pages.

Mariete tirelessly offered detailed explanations of all the pictures and spoke about all the marital tragedies in animated tones. Including that of her own parents. As a wealthy and beautiful girl, her mother had wanted to marry a man who was far below her station, a "bald schoolteacher." Mariete told him that her mother still wore a gold ring with a strand of his hair twisted around it, though she claimed that the hair was from one of her grandmothers. She had never felt anything but contempt for Van 't Westeinde, whom she called a "pipsqueak" when he had come courting.

Purplish, stiff photographs nevertheless showed Camiel's father to be a handsome youth, dressed in light sporty clothes, while his peers were all portrayed in stiff, black worsted jerkins and velvet trousers.

"Mother wasn't allowed to marry the schoolmaster, and after endless quarreling she wound up with father after all."

"I don't think they even cared about each other. They were always fighting, and we're the product of the reconciliations. Mother was the first to have an affair, and right afterwards father went out and did the same. We're all legitimate, but there are quite a few little Van 't Westeindes running around under different names.

"The odd thing is that they've learned to tolerate and even appreciate each other, though they never go out together. The first and last time they tried, they drove into a tree. Father wound up with a concussion, and mother's leg has never healed, but since then there's been peace in the house, and everybody does their own thing.

"When we were little, it was hell. God, we were so scared all the time. There was nowhere we could go to ask for help.

"Father's eyes would blaze. He would make wild threats, while mother stood tall and unflinching on the other side of the table, the bread knife in her hand. Then we would run outside, crying to the rabbits or the pigeons. Camiel was always inconsolable . . ."

Her eyes filled with tears, and for the first time Ed felt sympathy for her. This time it was real.

"I'm the oldest, and you know me a bit now. Then comes Magdalena, who ran away with nothing but her pretty face and her good figure. Corrie is in an institution, and Camiel isn't normal either. I'm the worst. I'm dangerous. I like you, and at the moment I'm being sincere. That's why I beg you: leave here before it's too late. You don't know what I'm capable of!"

She proudly wiped away her tears.

Ed was startled by the tone of her words, but he put his arm around her.

"That's nonsense, Mariete. You're just upset from all the memories." She resisted.

"Don't you believe me? Shall I prove it to you?" she asked recklessly.

He had the feeling she wanted to tell a secret, but since he couldn't imagine that it could *really* be anything serious, he shook his head with a smile and kissed her eyes, which were still damp.

The photo albums slid onto the floor, and their embrace became more intimate than he had intended.

Ed felt the same sense of panic he had felt the last time.

"Come with me, to Camiel's room," she whispered, and fatefully, Ed couldn't think of any words that would help him out of the situation. With a blunt refusal he left the room. At the doorway he turned around, struck by a stabbing pain in the back of his head.

It was Mariete's gaze, so laden with hostility that he came back to her, defeated.

But she bent down as if she hadn't noticed and picked up the albums.

She was wearing ugly garters, just above the knees.

Eleven

Plowing requires a certain amount of skill, and digging up beets proved to be too strenuous for Ed. He looked on with envy as Camiel made perfectly straight furrows in the rich black clay, the polder wind in his hair, the seagulls screaming behind him, while he, Ed, went into the stinking feed lot, where the cattle were fattened up, to shovel out the manure gutters and put fresh straw under the animals.

The land Camiel was plowing bordered on the pasture on which the feed lot stood, and sometimes he would come by to talk after a few passes, if the horses needed a rest.

A few days had passed since Camiel's "confession." He seemed calmer, and as far as Ed could tell, the nighttime attacks had also stopped. Ed envied his secure future, the quiet, uncomplicated life that lay before him. Free, the plow in his hand, the ropes, the white horses tamed in his strong fist. Before him lay the rich polderland, where the winds were born. A rich, fertile farm, of which he would be lord and master when the war was over, helped by a strapping young wife who would bring him peace and brush the memory of all past misery from his forehead.

And what would happen to *him*? They were all still young, weren't they?

Sometimes Ed would tell him stories about what the future would be like, and then he would share in Camiel's fantasies. In his childlike way Camiel planned to set aside a lot of the money he would earn in order to help Ed get his start as a writer, and Ed accepted it, so as not to disturb his sunny illusions.

Later, when he thought back on it, it seemed to him that the landscape was bathed in a heavenly glow, even though ominous storm clouds were gathering above.

Ed never knew the real cause, but his intuition told him that it was all Mariete's fault.

Among the calves in the barn, the mood between them became almost unbearable. Ed watched how the low sunlight came in through the dusty window panes and stroked their rough red and black backs. Specks of dust and straw particles danced in the sunbeams and the pleasant smell of clean straw rose up from the floor. The lowing cows turned their heads towards the door as Mariete came in with buckets of skimmed milk. He helped her carry them and feed the animals.

Sniffing greedily, the calves dipped their shiny snouts into the foamy milk.

It seemed that the peace had been signed, but the defeat had not been forgotten. For Mariete, Ed no longer existed. At least she acted as if he didn't, but she seemed to be sleepwalking.

He was beginning to get quite scared of her, and he decided that the sensible thing to do would be to leave the farm as soon as possible.

Camiel? He would have to leave him because of this wretched girl. He had his doubts. Maybe everything would sort itself out, but he knew he was kidding himself. He had to get away.

But where could he go? He saw Mrs. Van 't Westeinde come home and then her husband. He wanted to ask their advice, but he dawdled in the barn. It was too difficult.

Later he saw Mariete again after she had apparently just returned from a bicycle trip, and Camiel, who was taking the horses to the watering hole in the pasture before stabling them for the night.

He waited until he came; he would have to tell him.

Camiel's face darkened, and Ed noticed that he did not take his concerns lightly.

"I wouldn't put anything past Mariete. She's a bad egg. It's not nice to say that about your own sister. It's best you leave this evening, when it's dark, instead of going to bed. Wait for me by the fence at the orchard. I'll bring you to one of my uncles, and we'll take it from there. I don't trust Mariete as far as I can throw her. I'm almost sure she has a Kraut boyfriend on the side. I've noticed things, heard things more than once. I don't know, it's like you can feel her spying on you, thwarting you at every turn. I never wanted to say anything because of my friendship with Ernst. I'm sure you can understand.

"So I'll see you tonight. If nothing happens here, I'll give you a signal, and you can come back after a few days."

Ed thought his suggestion was bold and sensible.

He felt defeated, unhappy, but also resentful. Couldn't they have found a safe house for him that was a bit more . . . safe? With fewer nutcases and above all fewer German complications? He realized that parents were not responsible for the actions of their grown children. But still.

Mariete—if it was her fault—was too quick for him.

Dinner was still on the table when they heard loud knocking at the back and the front door at the same time. A moment later the Grüne Polizei were in the room.

If Mariete was playacting, she was a consummate performer.

She was practically the only one to speak. She swore; she was threatened. She even defended Ed.

Van 't Westeinde and his wife sat there at the table, frozen in their chairs, the very picture of powerless indignation, not thinking for a second of their own interests.

While the Germans concentrated on Mariete, who was carrying on like a woman possessed, Camiel quickly led Ed down a trapdoor to the cellar.

The long cellar that ran under the entire house had two small, moldered windows at the end, just above the ground.

They pushed one of them in and squeezed their way outside onto the gravel path in front of the house.

The Germans who had stayed outside and were posted at various points around the property did not see them in time. They fired at the hunched-over figures as they ran away. Ed saw Camiel fall to the ground, face first. He felt himself get hit in the shoulder, but he kept on running.

He got away.

Twelve

Almost two years later, on an August evening Eduard van Wyngen returned to Kruisdorpe.

A letter he had written had gone unanswered. The Van 't Westeindes were not writers; he knew that, and he decided to go visit the family, to thank them and hear how they had fared.

He was glad the sun was already setting and no one would recognize him before he got to the farm.

The badly mutilated silhouette of the old church of Kruisdorpe rose up against the pale evening sky, and it was clear from the streets as well that the liberation had ravaged this little village. He walked down the lane even more hesitantly and slowly than the first time.

Shell fragments had stripped and disfigured the beautiful treetops. Their branches were giant, ugly talons clawing at the sky.

The little bridge was gone. It had been replaced by a primitive wooden platform, which was already broken and cracked.

Sour smells from the ripe wheat fields and bitter-sweet scents from the orchard, which was alive with chirping crickets, intoxicated him with memories.

Startled, Ed stopped dead in his tracks.

In the dusky lane a strange figure was spinning around and around and around, waving his arms like the blades of a windmill.

It was a young man, dressed in the tattered remnants of a German uniform, his cap pulled down deep over his eyes.

When he saw Ed, he stopped waving his arms.

He was drooling and hiccupping, and he went over and leaned up against a tree. There was something exotic about him. Wild salt-and-pepper curls, which hadn't been cut in some time, protruded from his cap.

Was this the village idiot, one of the Van 't Westeinde's many crazy cousins? Did he belong here?

Ed overcame his revulsion and walked up to the figure, somewhat anxiously.

"I'm looking for Mr. Van 't Westeinde."

"Grrr—gesture of someone being hanged—*kaput*!"

"Mrs. Van 't Westeinde, Mariete?"

The lunatic made an obscene gesture, put his hand up to his own throat and said, "Tscht—*kaput!*"

"Camiel?"

"Ca-miel?" the figure repeated in a sing-song voice.

He stretched out his shoulders and deliberately, almost devoutly, began fumbling around in the inside pocket of the torn jacket of his uniform.

He took out a wallet and handed Ed a grubby, folded piece of paper.

Then he started to laugh, a barking laugh, and began running down the lane, waving his arms all the while and bellowing, "Kaput, alles, kaput, alles kaput!"

Ed tucked away the paper and forced himself to continue walking.

When he reached the property he saw the devastation in the hesitant light.

Fragments of walls and scorched beams jutting out of black ash heaps were all that was left of the farm.

A pale moon drifted freely between the clouds. It illuminated the desolate landscape with an ashen light before disappearing again.

All that remained of the four lindens were the stumps, from which young, leafy branches grew.

He sat down on one of the stumps and let the light of his flashlight play across the ruins of the house.

The thick layer of ash still gave off a bitter smell.

He stumbled through it to reach the only standing interior wall, which was holding up a half-collapsed chimney. A white cat scurried through the rubble.

There, blistered by the fire and covered in soot, stood the angel of hope in her green garment, the golden anchor in her hand. Her head with its sublime gaze had been burned off, but at her feet, Eben-Haezer remained as before: vaguely legible, with the word *Hope* running through it.

Ed cursed and threw a stone at those words. It only made his hands dirty with wet ash. After a while he switched on the flashlight again and unfolded the paper the madman had handed him with such solemnity.

The page was covered in typically German handwriting and torn at the folds. There was a dark brown bloodstain on it, and it was missing a corner.

He read:

> du hast mich an dinge gemahnet
> die heimlich in mir sind
> du warst für die saiten der seele
> der nächtige flüsternde wind
> und wie das rästelhafte,
> das rufen der atmenden nacht
> wenn draußen
> und man
> zu

> [you reminded me of things
> which are secretly inside me
> for the strings of my soul you were
> whispers of the night wind
> and like that mystery,
> the call of the breathing night
> when outside
> and one
> to]